KAT KONG

W9-BHX-624

Starring FLASH, RABIES, *and* DWAYNE
and introducing BLUEBERRY *as the Monster*

Written and directed by

DAV PILKEY

SCHOLASTIC INC.
New York Toronto London Auckland Sydney

No part of this publication may be reproduced in whole or in part, or stored in a retrieval system, or transmitted in any form or by any means, electronic, mechanical, photocopying, recording, or otherwise, without written permission of the publisher. For information regarding permission, write to Permissions Department, Harcourt Brace & Company, 8th Floor, Orlando, FL 32887.

ISBN 0-590-48761-2

Copyright © 1993 by Dav Pilkey.
All rights reserved. Published by Scholastic Inc., 555 Broadway, New York, NY 10012, by arrangement with Harcourt Brace & Company.

4 3 2 1   04 05 06

Printed in the U.S.A.   40
First Scholastic printing, February 1995

The illustrations in this book are manipulated photographic collage, heavily retouched with acrylic paint.

Starring

FLASH
*as Professor
Vincent Varmint*

RABIES
as Rosie Rodent

DWAYNE
*as Captain
Charles Limburger*

BLUEBERRY
as the Monster

For NATE HOWARD,
who tamed the savage kitty

TS	THIS BOOK HAS BEEN RATED
	TERRIBLY SILLY
	Some material may be too silly for grown-ups.

All the animals used in these photographs are the author's pets.
No harm came to them in the making of this book.

One dark and perilous night, three mouse explorers sailed toward a strange, uncharted island.

Captain Charles Limburger steered the tiny vessel,
while Doctor Vincent Varmint and his beautiful assistant,
Rosie Rodent, looked on.

When they reached the island, the three explorers were astonished. A group of natives was performing an ancient ceremony, offering up a sacrificial can of tuna fish and repeating a mysterious chant:

"Heeeer, Ki-tee Ki-tee!

Heeeer, Ki-tee Ki-tee!

Heeeer, Ki-tee Ki-tee Ki-tee!"

Suddenly, the island began to tremble.

Crashing through the thick forest came the most frightening creature ever known to mousekind: the mighty Kat Kong!

Meowing and hissing ferociously, the colossal cat took three giant kitty steps . . .

. . . and tripped over the tuna fish can. Klunk!
Kat Kong bumped his head on the ground and was
knocked out cold.

"If only we could bring him back to the city with us," said Doctor Varmint.

"No," replied Rosie Rodent, "it would be wrong to take this creature away from its natural habitat just to satisfy our scientific curiosity."

"Forget science," squeaked Doctor Varmint. "Think of the money we could make!"

So the three explorers wrapped Kat Kong in a giant burlap bag and tied him tightly to the ship.

As they sailed back to the great city of Mousopolis, they took special care not to let the cat out of the bag.

Several days later in downtown Mousopolis, Doctor Varmint unveiled his discovery to a sold-out crowd.

"Ladies and gentlemice," he squeaked. "I give you Kat Kong: the nine-lived wonder of the world!"

The audience cheered.

Kat Kong, however, was not amused. The towering tomcat hissed and meowed wildly.

"Do not be afraid," Doctor Varmint told the crowd.

"There is no way this creature can escape!"

"I repeat—there is NO WAY this creature can escape!...

Well, aah—actually, I *could* be wrong about that."

Soon, the city of Mousopolis was in a panic. The ferocious feline tore through the streets, knocking down buildings, ripping out power lines, and generally causing quite a ruckus!

Captain Charles Limburger rushed off to organize a
counterattack team, while the beautiful Rosie Rodent
watched the destruction from her apartment window.
"Help!" cried the engineer. "The cat's got my train!"

"Help!" squeaked the butcher. "The cat's got my tongue!"

"Help!" shrieked Rosie. "The cat's got me!"

Soon the crazed cat was heading straight for the top
of the Romano Inn . . .

. . . with the beautiful Rosie tailing behind.

A fleet of airplanes quickly flew into action, but their weapons were useless against the meowing menace. It seemed as if *nothing* could stop the terrifying Kat Kong.

Then, suddenly, a squeaking ray of hope rocketed through the thick clouds of gloom and despair. Captain Charles Limburger to the rescue!

Captain Limburger had a plan. He swooped close to Kat Kong and held out a red package tied with gold ribbons.

"Hey, Kat!" he shouted. "Look what I've got!"

He circled again and again shouting, "You'll never guess what's inside this package!"

"And he can't get up," said another.

"Well," said the chief of police, "It looks as if beauty killed the beast!"

"No," said Doctor Varmint as he looked sadly into the glowing red horizon. "It was curiosity. Curiosity killed the cat!"